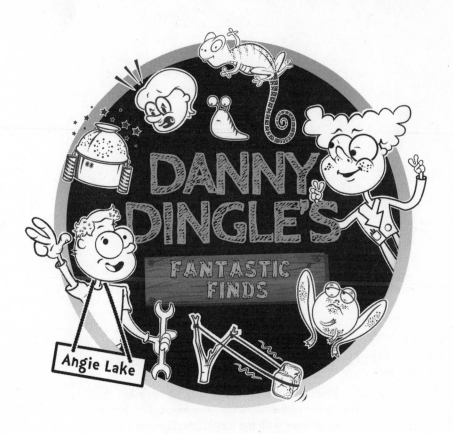

DANNY DINGLE'S

FANTASTIC FINDS

Angie Lake

The Mighty
Iron Foot

Published by Sweet Cherry Publishing Limited
Unit 36, Vulcan House
Vulcan Road
Leicester, LE5 3EF
United Kingdom

www.sweetcherrypublishing.com

First published in the UK in 2018
ISBN: 978-1-78226-262-6

1 3 5 7 9 10 8 6 4 2

Danny Dingle's Fantastic Finds: The Mighty Iron Foot

Printed and bound in Inida by Thomson Press India Ltd.

DANNY DINGLE'S

FANTASTIC FINDS

Book 4

The Mighty Iron Foot

Written by Angie Lake
Illustrated by Shanith MM and Suruchi Sati

DANNY DiNGLE'S SUPER-SECRET SPY NOTEBOOK.

ABSOLUTELY DO NOT READ (unless you are Danny, Percy or Superdog.)

NOTE: If you are not Danny, Percy or Superdog ... I have attached the world's **SMELLIEST SOCK** to the next page.

It's one of Percy's camping socks which has been sitting in the corner of the clubhouse for two months containing a rather slimy, rather mouldy, raw onion.

Continue at your own risk! You have been **warned** ...

It's enough to make anyone **SICK**, isn't it?

OK, so by now you probably know a few things about me, seeing as I'm a **world-famous, top-secret** inventor.

My assistant Percy and I are both GENIUS inventors who make C☺☺L STUFF out of the fantastic finds we make on our travels.

This wouldn't be possible without the help of the talented and telepathic **SUPERDOG**.

BZZZ...

Percy and I each have our own special **inventor's kit** that we carry around with us at all times. This kit includes:

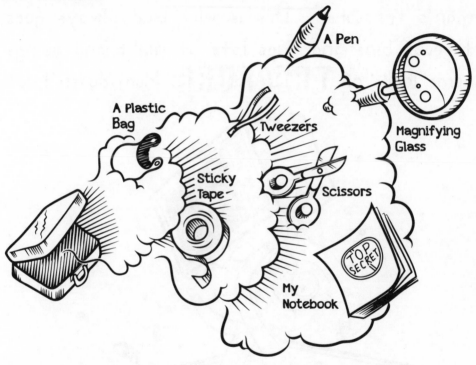

This way we can examine, pick up, chop off, carry and write down all of our **COOL FINDS**. You never know when you're going to find something really useful!

Percy and I are always on the lookout for **COOL STUFF**. Dad, who is also a genius inventor (like me), says that "One man's junk is another man's treasure". This is why Dad always goes through bins and skips late at night and brings home loads of **TREASURE**. Mum doesn't let

Dad keep his treasure in the house though, so for years he has been **VERY UNFAIRLY** forced to keep all the broken microwaves, bits of old tiles and smashed-up furniture in the garage.

This is why, for years, Mum and Dad have had to park their cars in the front garden. We had to cement over the fish pond last year to make more room for everything.

Anyway, Percy and I aren't allowed to keep our **FANTASTIC FINDS** in the house either, but we have a Top-Secret Laboratory — cleverly disguised as a clubhouse — where we keep all of our **COOL STUFF**. (Keep that to yourself, though, it's a SECRET!)

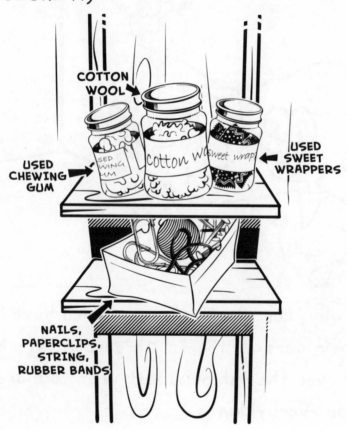

COTTON WOOL

USED SWEET WRAPPERS

USED CHEWING GUM

NAILS, PAPERCLIPS, STRING, RUBBER BANDS

Anyway, Percy and I went through the bins behind Henry's Hardware last weekend and we made the following **AWESOME** fantastic finds:

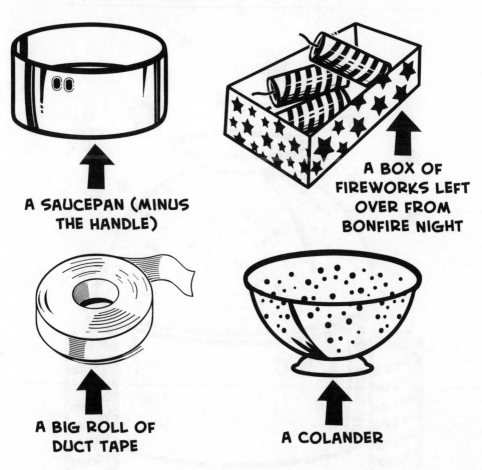

A SAUCEPAN (MINUS THE HANDLE)

A BOX OF FIREWORKS LEFT OVER FROM BONFIRE NIGHT

A BIG ROLL OF DUCT TAPE

A COLANDER

'What can you make with this?' I hear you ask ...

Well, BEHOLD!

AN UNIDENTIFIED FLYING POPCORN POPPER!

At first Percy and I were going to make a normal UFO, but Dad suggested putting some un-popped popcorn in it.

With the **FIREWORKS** and the popcorn it makes quite a racket. This makes it even COOLER, if you ask me.

The only real problem that we've found with it is that we never know where it's going to land.

Mrs Bergenstein wasn't very happy when it landed in her FISH POND.

And the popcorn did go a bit **soggy** ...

We still ate it, though.

But Mum stopped us from playing with it when Mr Higgings, who used to be in the army, had to be hospitalised. He thought he was under **ENEMY FIRE** and had a panic attack.

YOU'LL NEVER TAKE ME ALIVE!!

AMBULANCE

It was **hilarious** (even though Mum didn't seem to think so). Mum doesn't seem to appreciate my fantastic inventing skills or my **AWESOME** sense of humour.

Dad was out at the time, but I just had to tell **someone** about it, so I called Grandad Leonard and Granny Jean.

They're **REALLY** into science-fiction, so I knew they'd be in AWE of my fabulous UFO.

Grandad has been going on, and on ...

For ages and ages, and ages, and ages, and ages,
and ages, and ages, and ages, and ages, and ages,
and ages, and ages, and ages, and ages, and ages,
and ages, and ages, and ages, and ages, and ages,
and ages, and ages, and ages, and ages, and ages,
and ages, and ages, and ages, and ages, and ages,
and ages, and ages, and ages, and ages, and ages,
and ages, and ages, and ages, and ages, and ages,
and ages, and ages, and ages, and ages, and ages,
and ages, and ages, and ages, and ages, and ages,
and ages, and ages, and ages, and ages, and ages,
and ages, and ages, and ages, and ages, and ages,
and ages, and ages, and ages, and ages, and ages,
and ages, and ages, and ages, and ages, and ages,
and ages, and ages, and ages, and ages, and ages,
and ages, and ages, and ages, and ages, and ages,
and ages, and ages, and ages, and ages, and ages,
and ages, and ages, and ages, and ages, and ages,
and ages, and ages ... (YOU GET THE IDEA!)

about how we should build him a **FREEZE RAY** like the ones he sees in his alien invasion movies.

Apparently a **FREEZE RAY** is a kind of gun that emits a beam and anything that gets trapped in the beam freezes and can't move.

We had already designed Grandad a heat ray, which **MELTS** things. We demonstrated this by melting some cheese onto a slice of toast.

Grandad said that it was very **CREATIVE**, but that we should probably give Mum her hairdryer back before we got told off and get back to work on the **FREEZE RAY**.

Percy and I went back into the clubhouse to see what we could make a freeze ray out of. This is what we came up with:

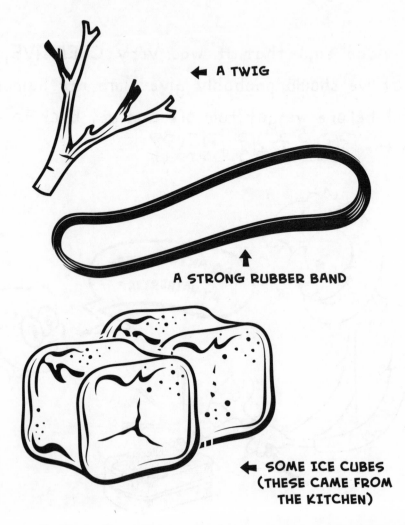

← A TWIG

↑
A STRONG RUBBER BAND

← SOME ICE CUBES
(THESE CAME FROM
THE KITCHEN)

From all of these things we built a fully functional
FREEZE RAY!!

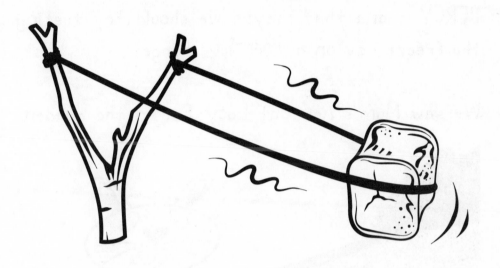

We needed to find something to test it on, so
we tested it on the fence, on a tree and on the
ground.

It **SEEMED** to be working: they didn't move at all
after the ice cube hit them!

Percy did point out that all of those things would have remained perfectly still whether they had been hit by the freeze ray or not – THANKS, PERCY – and that maybe we should try testing the freeze ray on a moving target.

We saw Mum's new cat Lucy-Fur in the garden.

Mum adopted Lucy-Fur a few weeks ago:

It was a Tuesday morning, just before dawn. It had been a restless night for the Dingle family. We'd all been kept awake by **CREEPY** and **SUSPICIOUS** banging noises.

BANG! BANG!

Dad said that it was probably GHOSTS. Mum said that it was probably rats in the garage, nesting in Dad's pile of rubbish. I thought they were probably both right and that Dad's treasure was haunted by evil **GHOST RATS!**

I couldn't help but think what a great addition to our **SUPERHERO-GENIUS-SPY-INVENTOR** team a ghost rat would be. And a whole army of ghost rats? We could rule the world! I mean, I'm not sure how exactly ... but I know that my enemies would **TREMBLE** in their trainers at the sight of me and my army of loyal ghost rats!

We crept into the garage, half expecting to see hundreds of ghost rats, their eyes glowing in the dark. But the truth was far more **TERRIFYING** than that ...

Mum opened the door and we stood in silence.

Suddenly, we heard a very faint **MEWING** coming from inside a microwave that Dad had brought back from a skip. I went over and opened

the door and Lucy-Fur **STREAKED** past me. She jumped straight into Mum's arms, and snuggled up to her. THEN she slowly turned her head, shot me and Dad an EVIL GLARE and hissed at Superdog.

At this moment I saw that the cat had chosen her side, and it wasn't the side of the genius superhero inventors. The cat could **NOT** be trusted. I tried to warn Mum that Lucy-Fur was evil, but it was too late: she had fallen madly in love with the DEMONIC FLEABAG.

Lucy-Fur was here to stay.

But anyway, none of that has anything to do with our decision to try the freeze ray on Lucy-Fur. Really, we were just giving her a second chance. Maybe if we involved her in our **experiments**, she'd take our side instead.

Percy and I took a shot at her from the clubhouse, but she bolted away like **greased lightning**. We decided to look for a moving target that didn't run quite as fast.

Luckily, I remembered that my neighbour Mr Nesbit had converted his shed into a reptile house.

He keeps all sorts of **COOL REPTILES** in there. Some of them even win competitions!

It seemed only **LOGICAL** to sneak into his garden and creep into the reptile house.

Mr Nesbit had some very **interesting** animals in the shed: there were lots of different kinds of snakes, lizards and iguanas.

We had to choose a target though, so we took aim at Mr Nesbit's PRIZE-WINNING showjumping chameleon.

We pointed the freeze ray at it and took a shot, but we missed it ...

Or at least we **THiNK** we missed it ...

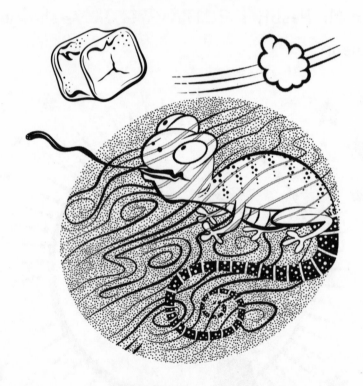

The chameleon **CHANGED COLOUR** and we couldn't see it anymore.

After that we hung out in the **REPTILE SHED** for a bit, just shooting cubes around. One of them hit Percy.

Percy **DIDN'T** freeze.

BUT he did point out that the ice cubes might end up hurting the animals and that we should probably stop it and come up with a better plan.

We were just about to leave the reptile shed when I looked down and noticed ...

OH, NO!! DISASTER!!

One of our ice cubes had landed on what looked like a chameleon's nest and **broken** all the eggs!

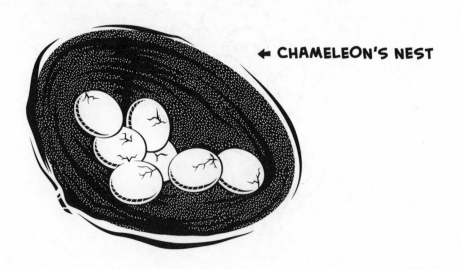

← CHAMELEON'S NEST

Percy and I looked at the nest, then at each other, then at the nest again ...

We knew we would be in **HUGE** (and I do mean
HUGE!!!!!) trouble if anyone found out about this.

We **HATCHED** a plan. (Ha ha ... get it? Eggs?
Hatch ...? Okay, maybe it's not very funny under
the circumstances.)

I rushed into the kitchen to look for some *hen's
eggs.*

Percy rushed into the garden to look for some hedgehog eggs.

We met up back at Mr Nesbit's **reptile house**. Things weren't going well:

The hen's eggs were all **WAY** too big. As for Percy's idea – it turns out that hedgehogs don't even lay eggs! (Nice thinking, Percy!)

I was sure we were **DOOMED** until I looked up and spotted a bird's nest in a tree. I got a ladder and **VERY CAREFULLY** handed the eggs down to Percy.

They looked to be EGGSactly the right size.

Now all we had to do was replace the broken chameleon eggs with bird eggs and nobody would **EVER** know the difference.

Percy and I snuck secretly – **TOP SECRETLY** – back into Mr Nesbit's reptile house (which wasn't difficult as we'd left the door wide open). We carefully replaced the squashed chameleon eggs with the bird's eggs and stepped back to admire our handiwork ... THE PERFECT CRIME!

(We felt pretty **EGG**cellent about it – haha!)

We were just breathing a sigh of relief when, out of the corner of my eye, I spotted Lucy-Fur running out of the door with what looked like a dead **PRIZE-WINNING CHAMELEON** in her mouth.

We shot out of the reptile house and followed Lucy-Fur as she made her way towards the cat flap in our kitchen door, DETERMINED to take Mum her offering: Mr Nesbit's dead chameleon.

We had to act quickly. I knew from experience that it would take Mum seconds to come to the conclusion that it was all our fault. Mum ALWAYS comes to the conclusion that things are our fault. She should think about that. After all, there *is* a chance that one day she might be wrong.

44

Percy thought fast: he took the freeze ray and started shooting ice cubes at Lucy-Fur.

The plan worked! Lucy dropped the chameleon and ran off.

Percy and I then **RUSHED** over to inspect the chameleon.
We examined the chameleon for signs of life. There weren't many.

No, that's a lie: there weren't **ANY.**

We realised that the only thing we could do was put the chameleon back in the reptile house (trying our best to cover any bits that Mum's EVIL cat had chewed), close the reptile house door (properly this time!) and **NEVER, EVER** speak of this again.

Percy and I decided that the rest of the afternoon should be spent hiding (SECRETLY) in the ~~secret lab~~ clubhouse.

That's where we came up with our next **GENIUS** idea. (We were really having a good day as far as coming up with **GENIUS IDEAS** was concerned!!)

We realised that a lot of our super-secret inventor's work can be really DANGEROUS. I mean, **some** people complain that we're a menace to our neighbours and their pets, but I think that actually THEY'RE dangerous to US. (If we get caught.)

We realised that, with our clubhouse being in a tree, we should definitely think of an emergency escape route in case we ever have to leave in a hurry.

We came up with the following options:

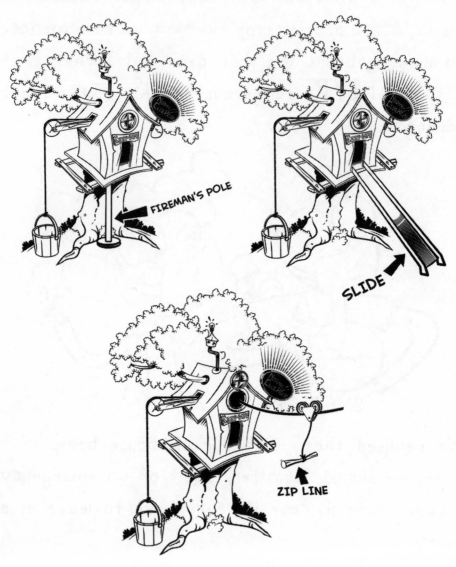

FIREMAN'S POLE

SLIDE

ZIP LINE

In the end we decided that the easiest thing would be to borrow Mum and Dad's mattress so we could jump to safety.

We were just indoors, trying to get the mattress down the stairs when she BUSTED us.

At that moment the doorbell rang and I breathed
a sigh of relief.

Getting the mattress back up the stairs was much less fun than taking it downstairs.

In any case, this wasn't looking good for us: "Wait for me in the kitchen," she'd said. Mum likes to tell me off in the kitchen. I mean, she likes telling me off in a lot of places, but the kitchen is by far one of her **favourite** places to do it in.

We put the mattress back, and then, while we waited for Mum, we decided to scoff a bit of Dad's latest batch of herring, hummus and hot chilli fart jelly ...

 FARTASTIC!

Mum looked cross when she walked into the kitchen.

The conversation went very much like this:

I kicked Percy under the table.

I had to admit that Mum had a bit of a point.

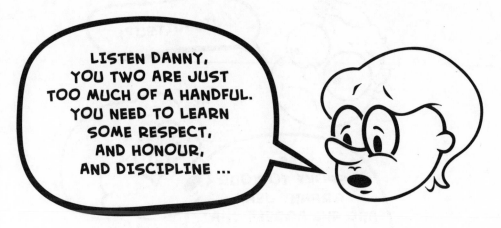

I DID **NOT** LIKE WHERE THIS WAS GOING.

... JIU-JITSU?!

YES.
I SPOKE TO YOUR GRANNY JEAN AND SHE AGREES THAT MARTIAL ARTS WOULD HELP GET YOU OUT OF THE HOUSE. I THINK IT WILL PROVIDE YOU WITH EXERCISE AND KEEP YOU OUT OF TROUBLE.

Normally I **BEG** Mum not to make me do this kind of stuff, but actually jiu-jitsu could be perfect superhero training. If I get good I could become Metal Face's sidekick. (Metal Face is the world's biggest and most FARTACULAR superhero!)

I've come up with a name and everything!

Behold the mighty ...

EXPERIMENTAL FACE!

If I learn **JIU-JITSU**, not only would I come up with awesome inventions, but I would also be able to break bricks and bits of wood with my head, which is an incredibly **useful** skill to have.

This seems like a pretty flawless plan!

Percy and I were both pretty **HYPED** to be going to jiu-jitsu after class.

We spent all day in school training by **karate-chopping** stuff in half:

- Pencils

- Rulers

- Sandwiches

We did nearly get detention for attempting to karate-chop Miss Quimby's DOUGHNUT in half though.

WHAT DO YOU THINK YOU'RE DOING? STEP AWAY FROM THE DOUGHNUT!

When we got to the gym after school, we discovered that a few kids from school were also there:

- **AMY ALMOND** and **DEBRA DERBY** (they both had orange belts)

- **NITTY NEIL** and **BELINDA** (they had yellow belts)

There were also a few other beginners, so Percy and I weren't the only ones.

Percy and I waited for the sensei to arrive. Granny Jean says that a **sensei** is usually a wise old man with a very long beard and walking stick made out of a tree branch. She also said that he's meant to show us the path to **WISDOM** and harmony through the practice of a traditional discipline. We didn't like the sound of that discipline bit, so we thought we'd try searching for the mystical path ourselves.

Percy and I walked all around the gym, but the only path we could see was through the back door. It didn't look very **harmonious**. It was full of gravel, weeds, empty cans and crisp packets. So we went and stood in formation with everyone else.

We couldn't wait to see what the first lesson would be ...

Spinning kicks?

Chopping bricks in haLf?

Jumping over waLLs?

I couldn't believe my eyes when the sensei walked in. **IT WAS MS MILLS!!!**

Ms Mills, the super-scary, super-fearsome PE teacher! Ms Mills, who has the face and personality of a **BULLDOG**! Ms Mills, who makes us do push-ups for fun (that's fun for **HER**, not for us)! Ms Mills, who can't tell the difference between a kids' PE class and military training!

What was she doing here?!

Ms Mills didn't mess around. First she made us all run around in circles, then she made us do it backwards, then we did it sideways. After that she made us drop to the floor and do push-ups.

THIS WAS NOTHING LIKE IN THE FILMS!

I was about to pretend to faint so I could leave the class (Why not? It always works in PE!) when suddenly she said:

OKAY, TODAY'S LESSON IS GOING TO BE ARMLOCKS.

I thought I'd give it a chance.

All of the other kids knew some basic armlocks, but Percy and I had no clue what to do.

Ms Mills explained that armlocks were a good way to make sure that a person couldn't get up again once we'd **PINNED** them down. She showed us how to get someone into an armlock on the floor, and how to put **pressure** on their elbow joint to keep them there.

NOW BOYS,
BE VERY CAREFUL.
WE DON'T WANT
ANY ACCIDENTS!

Percy and I **MESSED AROUND** and practiced while Ms Mills went to see how the other kids were getting on.

Percy and I had completely mastered the armlock by now. It was getting a bit **BORING**. z z z z z

I had Percy pinned to the floor by his left arm when suddenly, just behind his head, I spotted a shiny pound coin.

WHAT A FIND!!!

I guess I should have let Percy out of the armlock before diving for the coin, because the next thing I knew Percy was SCREAMING and I'd bent his elbow backwards.

Ms Mills was not happy. She had to call a paramedic. I was **confident** that everything would be OK.

So, maybe I was a bit **TOO** confident ...

I've learnt a **VALUABLE** lesson though: armlocks do work! Apparently Percy's arm is going to be in plaster for a few weeks.

When I got home that evening, Mum was **NOT** happy with me. She'd just been talking to Percy's mum. Percy had been banned from spending time with me.

I WAS GUTTED.

Who was going to help me classify all my **fantastic finds** now?

Who was going to help me with all my **C☀☀L** inventions?

Who was going to help me put things in jars? I mean, I couldn't see Percy taking the lids off the jars in his condition but we could have worked something out.

Who was going to sit with me in the clubhouse farting all evening? ... Well, apart from Dad?

This was a DISASTER!!!

And it was all Ms Mills' fault!!

I felt a little depressed as I catalogued my finds in the clubhouse that evening. Even they seemed less interesting without Percy there.

I'd found:

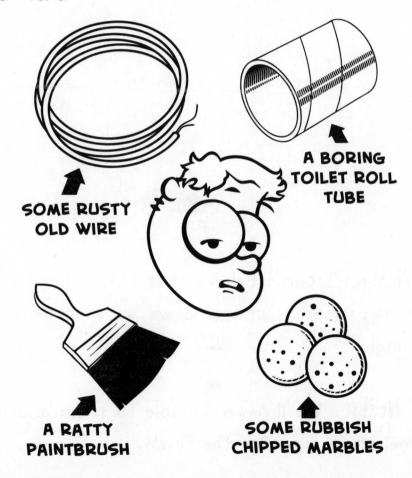

SOME RUSTY OLD WIRE

A BORING TOILET ROLL TUBE

A RATTY PAINTBRUSH

SOME RUBBISH CHIPPED MARBLES

There was no way I could make anything interesting with that, so I peered over the fence into Mr Nesbit's garden. The Nesbits were holding a funeral for **KARMA CHAMELEON**. They all looked really sad too.

Mr Nesbit: I can't believe that the championship is in two weeks' time, and we were so close to winning!

Mrs Nesbit: We'll never be able to train another chameleon in time for the finals.

They seemed really upset and I couldn't help but feel that maybe it was part of my **SUPERHERO** duty to help ... but how?

I looked over at **Superdog** ...

Superdog looked back over at me ...

At that moment I knew that we were thinking the **EXACT SAME THING.**

We were both thinking:

"With the right training and an **AWESOME** disguise, Superdog could pass for a showjumping chameleon, win the prize and save the day."

OF COURSE!! IT WAS SHEER GENIUS!!

Now all I needed to do was work on Superdog's disguise and make an obstacle course.

Superdog's disguise was quite easy. I had all the right bits:

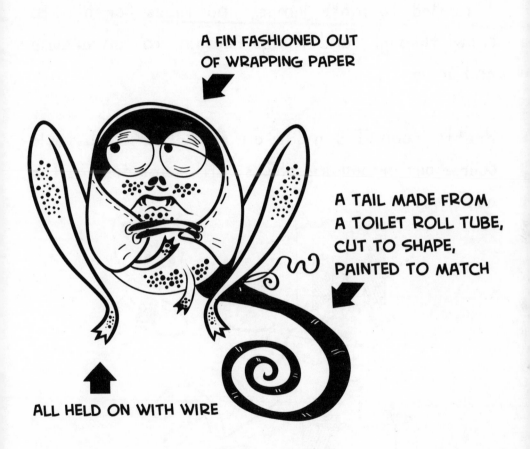

A FIN FASHIONED OUT OF WRAPPING PAPER

A TAIL MADE FROM A TOILET ROLL TUBE, CUT TO SHAPE, PAINTED TO MATCH

ALL HELD ON WITH WIRE

No one would ever know the difference. I thought he looked almost completely convincing!

Now I just had to make him an OBSTACLE COURSE.
To do this, I borrowed some of Baby Mel's toys.
I needed to make jumps, and tubes for him to
crawl through, and things for him to run around
and under ...

Pretty soon I'd made an **AWESOME** obstacle
course out of building blocks, with some dolls as the
audience.

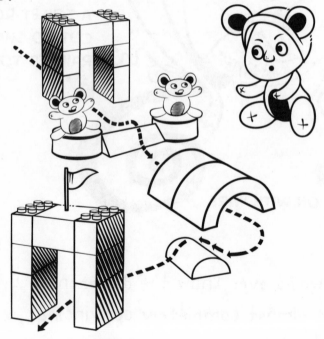

It wasn't easy to get Superdog to cooperate. He didn't seem as enthusiastic as you would expect considering this would be a ONCE-IN-A-LIFETIME opportunity to fine-tune his spy-training skills with my expertly engineered spy-training obstacle course. He seemed to need a lot of encouragement in the form of **dead insects**.

For a moment I was carried back to the times when Percy used to feed Superdog dead insects with me. Percy would **PUKE** ... Superdog would try to eat his sick ... Percy would puke some more ... I welled up a little, but then I remembered that I needed to be strong. For Karma Chameleon, and for chameleons everywhere!

The next day at school was AWKWARD.

I tried to talk to Percy when I arrived.

Percy wasn't talking to me. He looked at me coldly and showed me the **CAST** on his arm.

He seemed upset. Every time I tried to stand next to him, he walked away. I couldn't help but feel partly responsible (even though it was mostly Ms Mills' fault). I'd have to find a way to **APOLOGISE**.

At least Debra Derby was nice to me. She really understood my problems with Percy. She said that when she started jiu-jitsu she broke people's arms and legs all the time. She is **FREAKISHLY** strong, though.

I was happy for her sympathy, but I **secretly hoped** I'd never have to go up against her in jiu-jitsu ...

The only good part of the day was Science Club.
Mr Hammond was really excited. He said, "Now
kids, I'm really excited!" (Those were his exact
words.) "I have a big surprise for you!"

Mr Hammond wheeled a TV across the front the
room. The TV started playing some dramatic
music and then a voice said:

"Can your school stand up to the **ULTiMATE**
CHALLENGE?"

An **ULTiMATE CHALLENGE?** This was right up my street.

I sat up and looked around at my dopey classmates:

Neil and Belinda could barely rise to the challenge of keeping their **NITS** under control, Gareth was losing the challenge of not being the **world's biggest twit** and it was challenging for poor Percy to even keep his lunch down ...

I came to the conclusion that none of them would be of much help even in an easy challenge. Never mind something **ULTIMATE** like a zombie invasion or a super-intelligent gerbil mafia taking over the world.

(Well ... except maybe for Debra Derby and Amy Almond, I suppose they might have some **USEFUL SKILLS**.)

The voice continued:

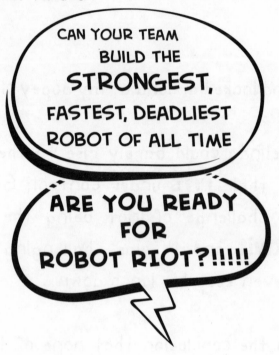

CAN YOUR TEAM BUILD THE **STRONGEST,** FASTEST, DEADLIEST ROBOT OF ALL TIME

ARE YOU READY FOR ROBOT RIOT?!!!!!

Then there were several minutes of home-made robots smashing each other up.

It was AWESOME!

Mr Hammond looked like he was about to cry with excitement by the time the video ended.

Everybody cheered. We didn't really understand what was going on, but we cheered anyway!

I had my doubts about it ... I mean, we had the enthusiasm, but what about the other stuff? Like the materials, the skills, the technical know-how, the experience ... you know ... **THE ROBOT??!!**

Luckily Mr Hammond had a plan. He told us that our first task was to get into groups of two and come up with a basic design. Then we'd look at all the ideas and see how we could make an AWESOME KILLER ROBOT out of them. He gave us each a copy of the DVD to study at home.

Now, I knew that I had a **MATHS EXAM** coming up ... so if I could put off studying for that by watching killer robots as homework instead, then killer robots it was!!

... Maths? UGH!!! I **HATE** maths!!!

It was like the decision had been made for me!

I was ready to head off home to enjoy an afternoon of **KILLER ROBOTS**. But as I left the classroom, I realised that I wouldn't be able to do this on my own. Part of my team was missing! Well, OK, I mean I probably COULD do all the work on my own, but I could really use Percy's company. He always tells me which of my ideas are the **BEST**.

I looked over at Percy.

Percy looked pointedly in the other direction.

I needed to fix this.

I waited until lunchtime. I sat next to Percy. He got up, picked up his tray with one hand (**sloshing** juice over everything), and moved to the next table. I watched him as I tucked into my **ANCHOVY AND PRUNE JELLY**.

First I watched him nibble at a **soggy baked bean sandwich,** spilling most of it down his shirt (which was buttoned wrong). It was a pretty poor choice of sandwich for someone who only has one working hand and is messy at the best of times: it kind of looked like he'd been **SICK** on himself again.

Then I watched him struggle to open his packet of crisps. This also seemed like another poor choice of food for someone with a broken arm. He tugged at the crumpled packet for a while before he eventually decided to sit on it until the bag BURST.

Then he just ate the crumbs. I couldn't help feeling a little sad about the whole thing. I love crisps — what a waste!

Danny: Err ... Percy ... I just wanted to say that I'm **really** sorry about your arm ...

Percy: Are you, Danny ... ARE YOU?

Danny: Yes. Yes I am.

Percy: How sorry?

Danny: Well ... remember that time I used your lunch box as a time capsule and **buried** it in the playground with your lunch in it and you fainted in class and everyone said it was because you were SCARED of the class goldfish?

Percy just ignored me and licked his finger to dab at more crumbs.

Danny: And I'm even more sorry than when we auditioned to be Metal Face's personal inventor and sidekick and I did a fart so epic you threw up in your helmet and Metal Face said "Superheroes need strong wind **and** strong stomachs!"

LIKE EXPERIMENTAL FACE HERE.

THAT NEVER HAPPENED . . .

Danny: Then how about that time I put CATNIP in your mum's bird feeder to see if cats really do always land on their feet?

Percy: ... That was you?

YOU'RE GROUNDED!

Danny: And why are we **obsessing** about who blew up what, or who might have lent who the wrong notes for that maths exam? This is **BIGGER** than us, Percy! This is about building the best killer robot the world (and ~~twit-faced~~ Gareth) has ever seen!

Danny: ... Plus, you know that **POUND COIN** I found in jiu-jitsu? Well, I've thought really hard about it and I've decided to share it with you.

Mum didn't seem very pleased with me when I got home. I think this is because:

- Percy had come with me to help with the **ROBOT DESIGN**, even though his mum didn't want us hanging out together anymore.

- We'd come straight home from school and forgotten about jiu-jitsu class. **(OOPS!)**

\-   I'd borrowed all of Baby Mel's *favourite* *toys* to make an obstacle course for Superdog.

\-   I'd tied the sofa cushions to a tree in the garden to practice my ▓▓▓▓▓ ▓▓▓▓ and left them outside overnight, in the rain ...

HEEE-YAAA!!!!

It didn't help that as soon as we got back, Mum's cat Lucy-Fur turned up at the back door with the dead chameleon she had dug up from next door's garden ... or that as soon as Percy saw this he was immediately **SICK** on the doorstep.

Why, Percy, **WHY???**

Percy and I decided that the best plan of action would be to grab some of Dad's new **EXPERIMENTAL** baked bean, corned beef and caviar jelly, and go straight up to my room to get to work on the plans for our robot.

Percy and I were faced with our most important challenge yet! To design a **killer robot** worthy of Metal Face.

First, and most importantly, the robot would need a really COOL name:

Hmm ... we'd have to think about this!

The robot would also need a really **COOL** weapon, like a big, double-headed axe or throwing stars.

Also, it would be **AWESOME** if the robot could fart. (I'm sure Dad could help with this bit.)

Percy and I worked away **all evening** and farted like we'd never been apart ...

Danny: Here comes a big one!!

Percy: I can make mine sound wet!

Danny: Are you sure that was just a fart?

And after a lot of hard work we came up with the design for the **best robot** in the history of history ...

BEHOLD THE MIGHTY IRON FOOT!

You'll never believe this. I may be delirious, I may have a fever, I may even have overdosed on Dad's AWESOME fart jelly, but ...

I really enjoyed school today!

Yes, I'll say it again: **I REALLY ENJOYED SCHOOL TODAY!**

I mean, it didn't start out promisingly. Most of the day was REALLY boring.

YAAAWNN!!!!

Miss Quimby was really annoyed with me for forgetting to do my English homework. (**OOPS!**) But actually I suspect that she was just grumpy because she hadn't had her MORNING DOUGHNUT.

(She **LOVES** doughnuts!)

She said that I'd have to write an essay on good versus evil in class.

I looked around me. Smug, full-of-himself, twit-faced Gareth Trumpshaw (my arch-rival and the biggest twit in history) was looking over at me and sniggering.

Gareth HAD remembered to do his homework. He always remembers to do his homework because he's not a **GENIUS INVENTOR** by night (and day) like me, and he has nothing better to do.

TWIT

GENIUS

Gareth turned to me when Miss Quimby wasn't looking and flashed his homework at me. There was a big A+ on the top of it.

He's such a **TWIT!!!**

I found a **CHEWED-UP** piece of chewing gum
under my desk and threw it at him. I missed.
It hit Miss Quimby's bum and got stuck there.
(**OOPS!**)

Fortunately she didn't notice.

PHEWWW!!!

I thought about my work for a bit, then I wrote an essay about **THE MIGHTY IRON FOOT**. It went like this:

Once upon a time (in the future) there was a smug evil twit called ... Gareth Dumpshaw. He thought he was really clever and that he knew everything about **EVERYTHING**, but he didn't because he was just a big, cheating twit.

DUMPSHAW = TWIT

The evil Gareth Dumpshaw wanted to take over the school and the world. He invented this potion to turn everyone into ZOMBIES. Well, HE didn't invent it: his dad invented it for him because his dad always helps him **cheat** at everything.

The evil Gareth Dumpshaw arrived at school early one morning and crept into the canteen where he was going to poison all the canteen food with his zombie potion. All the kids would be **DOOMED!**

But no! Fortunately for everyone there was one person who could save the day!

The world's biggest and best superhero:

EXPERIMENTAL FACE!

EXPERIMENTAL FACE had discovered Gareth Dumpshaw's evil plan and was waiting for him in the canteen.

Just as the evil Gareth Dumpshaw was about to pour some of his ZOMBiE POTiON in with the mashed potato, the awesome, super-strong and genius Experimental Face appeared before him.

Gareth Dumpshaw was terrified of the great **EXPERIMENTAL FACE.** He started shaking in fear, then he dropped the potion on the floor and peed himself.

He tried to run away.

"**YOU'LL NEVER ESCAPE!**" shouted the brave Experimental Face.

"YOU CAN'T STOP ME!" responded Dumpshaw.

He turned around, and he revealed that he had this **MASSIVE** jetpack on his back that his dad had probably made for him because he even has to cheat at being an evil villain.

It looked like Dumpshaw was going to escape out of a window, but Experimental Face had a **SECRET WEAPON** ...

Just as the Dumpshaw twit was trying to ignite his jetpack and fly away to freedom, the canteen **SHOOK** with an almighty roar.

The glass in the windows trembled as something that sounded like an **EARTHQUAKE** got louder and louder.

The canteen door burst open and there he was ... the biggest, scariest super robot of all time. It was Experimental Face's greatest invention:

THE MIGHTY IRON FOOT!

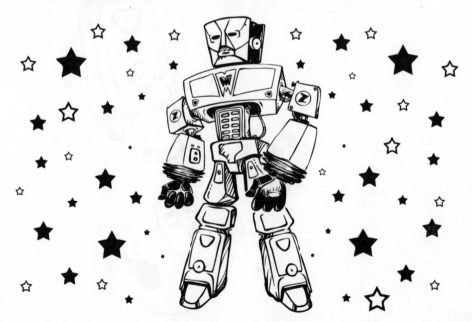

The Mighty Iron Foot got closer and closer, and the Dumpshaw twit peed himself in terror again. Then, just as it looked like Dumpshaw had got his jetpack to work, the Mighty Iron Foot grabbed him, threw him on the floor and used his enormous iron foot to squash Dumpshaw's big, fat, stupid head. And his brains came out (which wasn't much).

THE END.

Miss Quimby was really happy with my work. She said ...

WELL, IT'S BETTER THAN NOTHING.

RESULT!!!

I was so pleased about this that I didn't even worry about not having studied for my maths test ... but I was probably going to fail that anyway.

In the afternoon we had Science Club. Percy and I had been really looking forward to it.

I think we were all pretty excited about the **ROBOT RIOT** challenge. Everyone had brought drawings and designs of their robots.

Leo and Michael had teamed up and invented a robot called the **Super Scooper**.

It had fire as its main weapon and it also flung ice cream at its opponent.

We all liked the fire, but none of us agreed with wasting ice cream.

Leo's mum drives an ice-cream van, so they probably have lots of spare ice cream at home. Even so, there's no need to **WASTE** it!

Nitty Neil (who has nits yet again) and Belinda had designed **BLOODBATH WARRIOR**.

It was totally awesome, even though Mr Hammond said he wasn't too sure about the name.

It had a huge rotating disc saw that rose up and was supposed to saw the enemy robot in half.

I was really impressed with Debra Derby and Amy Almond's design: **THE GODDESS OF THUNDER.**

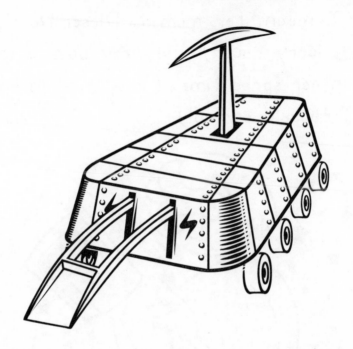

The robot could move **IN ANY DIRECTION**, and had heavy iron armour, a hydraulic arm for flipping the enemy robot and a **huge** ice pick that hammered down, making a hole in the other robot and **DAMAGING** all the electrics. They'd even brought blueprints.

Their team does have a clear advantage, though: Debra is an EXPERT at anything that has wheels (I mean, her mum is Diesel Doris, the **famous** lorry racer) and Amy does a lot of welding in her spare time. (Yes, it is an unusual hobby. I thought so too!)

Gareth Trumpshaw had decided to do the project on his own (as always). Why would he want to team up with us? He can just get his dad to come up with the design for him!

His robot, **BLADES OF FURY**, was really simple. It was just a flat robot with two blades that spun around really fast, ripping the enemy robots to pieces.

Mr Hammond said, "Wow, that's actually a really **efficient** design!" But he probably just felt sorry for Gareth and what he meant to say was:

"Your design is total **RUBBISH** and you are a total twit."

Mr Hammond had obviously decided to save the **BEST** till last ...

SO, PERCY AND DANNY,
WHAT HAVE YOU GOT FOR US?

Percy and I nodded at each other. Then we got out our drawing of **THE MIGHTY IRON FOOT!**

It had **TERRIFYING** flashing eyes, it could fly, and it said cool things like **"PREPARE TO MEET YOUR MAKER!"**

Gareth said that that didn't make any sense (he's such a **TWIT**).

Mr Hammond said he loved our robot.

THAT'S A VERY IMAGINATIVE DESIGN, BOYS!

But he had some technical queries:

AND WHAT DOES IT ACTUALLY DO?"

We explained.

IT HAS A BIG AXE . . .

AND IT FARTS...

Everyone must have been really impressed because the whole room went **REALLY** quiet.

Mr Hammond then said that he'd look at all the designs and see what ideas we could use to make the robot. Then he'd tell us the plan the following week.

Percy and I talked about our **AWESOME** design all the way to jiu-jitsu. You wouldn't think that Percy was in the best condition to do jiu-jitsu with a **BROKEN** arm, but his mum said that she'd paid for the whole month, so he should go and sit in the class and take notes.

We also kept a lookout for more **fantastic finds**. It was much less boring than when I was looking on my own. We found the following totally genius, amazingly **AWESOME** cool stuff:

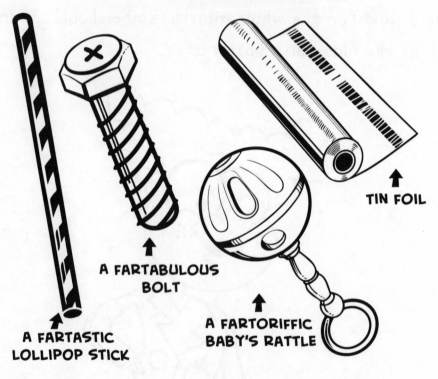

TIN FOIL

A FARTABULOUS BOLT

A FARTORIFFIC BABY'S RATTLE

A FARTASTIC LOLLIPOP STICK

I put everything into plastic bags that we carry with me in my **HANDY INVENTOR'S KIT** so that I could catalogue the finds later.

Jiu-jitsu was a little less **arm-breaky** than last time.

Ms Mills isn't JUST really scary, she also **REALLY** fancies Mr Hammond (the science teacher), and it turns out that she's found out about the **ROBOT RIOT** project.

As Percy can't do much in class since he broke his arm, Ms Mills has made him her **assistant**. Really this just means that she tries to get him to tell her as much information on Mr Hammond as possible.

WHAT WAS HE WEARING? WHEN WILL THE ROBOT COMPETITION TAKE PLACE? CAN YOU GET ME TICKETS? CAN YOU GET ME HIS NUMBER?

It's **PATHETIC.**

It's especially pathetic because I've been teamed up in class with Debra Derby, who is LOVELY – I mean that she is a lovely FRIEND. (I don't fancy her!!) But she is also freakishly strong. I'm covered in bruises!

Not that she's better at jiu-jitsu than me or anything, I just don't want to hurt her.

OK, who am I kidding? She's **WAY** better at jiu-jitsu than me!

Ms Mills spent the whole class trying to convince Percy that we should give our robot some jiu-jitsu moves. It may not be a bad idea, but I don't think Mr Hammond will go for it. Not if it means spending time with Ms Mills. He's **REALLY SCARED** of her.

I'm not surprised!

After jiu-jitsu we went straight back to the clubhouse to wait for Dad.

Dad was really excited about my idea to enter Superdog into the chameleon gymkhana (even though Superdog is not **TECHNICALLY** a chameleon).

Mum was not so pleased:

THE NEIGHBOURS HAVE SUFFERED ENOUGH; THEY DON'T NEED TO BE REMINDED ABOUT THAT POOR CHAMELEON EVERY FIVE MINUTES!

LOOK, DANNY IS JUST DOING THIS BY WAY OF AN APOLOGY, GWEN. I MEAN, IF YOU DON'T ALLOW HIM TO APOLOGISE FOR TRESPASSING, VANDALISM AND PET HOMICIDE BY DISGUISING A TOAD AS A CHAMELEON, WHAT MORAL MESSAGE ARE WE TEACHING DANNY EXACTLY?

Mum was just a bit cross. Apparently Mr Nesbit had visited because Lucy-Fur had been back to try and dig up **Karma Chameleon** yet again.

He was also confused as to why the ornamental eggs in the reptile house had hatched.

Apparently he is now the **PROUD DAD** of several sparrows that need feeding every fifteen to twenty minutes.

I knew that Mum would need some serious **buttering up** if she was going to let us take part in the gymkhana, but **FORTUNATELY** I'm resourceful ...

So I started with some *good old-fashioned nagging*:

Can we enter Superdog into the chameleon gymkhana, can we ... ?

Mum: Cut that out!

So I changed tactics and tried to convince her with a **little song**:

PLEASE MUM,
UNDERSTAND OUR MISSION.
WE MUST ENTER THE COMPETITION.
MR NESBIT'S HONOUR WE WILL DEFEND
AS HIS CHAMELEON CAME TO A STICKY END.

MUM, PLEASE DON'T STAND IN MY WAY.
LET SUPERDOG COME SAVE THE DAY
OR THE DINGLE HOUSEHOLD WILL ALWAYS REGRET
THAT OUR CAT CHEWED UP OUR NEIGHBOUR'S PET!

DANNY, THAT'S A HORRIBLE SONG!!

Mum didn't seem very convinced, although she eventually realised it would be good to have us out of the house for a day.

REEEEESULT!!!!!

Anyway, Dad was just as **excited** as me about Mum's answer, so he volunteered to help.

Dad's going to help me train Superdog AND he's going to bring along a new batch of fart jelly ...

GREAT NEWS! I'LL GET TO WORK ON A NEW BATCH OF FART JELLY!!

AWESOME!

SUPERDOG'S BIG DAY HAS FINALLY ARRIVED!

After days of intensive training:

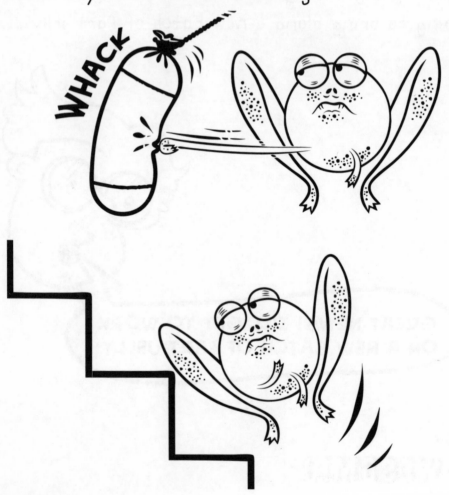

... and a lot of bribing with dead insects ...

... he is ready to show off his new skills at the **CHAMELEON GYMKHANA!!!**

If we'd had more time I would have trained a live insect to jump over the hurdles and go through the tubes so that Superdog could just follow it. But I am a **GENIUS**, not a MIRACLE WORKER: Superdog is as ready as he ever will be to take first place and leave the audience in awe.

Mum looked happy to wave us off as Dad, Superdog and I made our way to pick up Percy on the way to the village hall where **'Greenville's 7th Chameleon Gymkhana'** was being held.

We joined the line to sign up. Everyone's chameleons did look a bit more **CHAMELEONY** than Superdog, but we managed to get him past the enrolment process; even if Dad did nearly have a **HEART ATTACK** when he was told he'd have to pay fifty pounds to enter.

We watched some of the other chameleons warming up and practicing.

They seemed quite **graceful**.

Superdog doesn't really do anything gracefully; his style is a bit more 'drag your belly on the ground'. I think it's because his **telepathy** takes up a lot of his energy.

In any case we knew we'd be the best as we had a fresh batch of insects to help encourage Superdog over the jumps and around the obstacles.

We also had a fresh batch of **FART JELLY**, to help make the day more interesting.

Before the show started all the chameleons were given a number, then paraded and lined up.

Superdog did look a bit different from all the other chameleons ... and also kept trying to lick the other chameleons. I don't think they liked that. I know the owners **DEFINITELY** weren't impressed.

The judges gave us the basic rules:

It was an **obstacle course** with jumps, water jumps, tubes to go through and cones to go around. The chameleons would have to complete the course in a set order and the **WINNER** would be the chameleon that completed the course in the **fastest time**, in the right order and without knocking anything over.

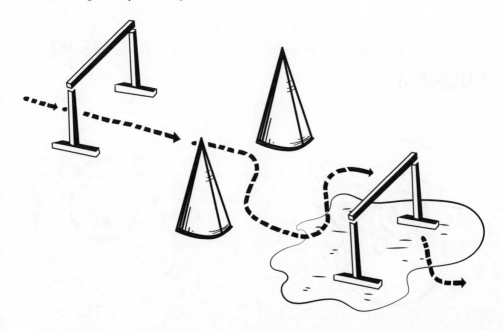

And then one of the judges said:

AND, OF COURSE, BRIBING THE CHAMELEONS AROUND THE COURSE WITH FOOD IS COMPLETELY FORBIDDEN.

OH NO!!! We hadn't thought about this. **WE WERE DOOMED!**

We watched and farted as one by one all the other chameleons gracefully completed the course in record time. My heart started to sink. So did Dad's – he'd paid **fifty pounds** to enter the competition.

Even so, I looked at Superdog and he seemed **CONFIDENT** ...

Or maybe he looked **indifferent.** (I can't always tell the difference.)

Superdog's turn came.

I placed Superdog at the start line of the obstacle course. Without the insect bribe we would have to rely on his incredible **PSYCHIC** powers to let him know what we wanted him to do.

We stood back and held our breath (and not just because our nervous farts had formed a **gassy cloud** around us).

Superdog stood there looking **blank** for a bit, then started pawing at the wrapping paper fin on his head trying to rip it off.

WHAT WAS HE DOING? He was going to totally blow his cover!!

Percy, Dad and I stood at the edge of the arena shouting words of encouragement:

Superdog didn't look remotely interested. He just looked **blankly** towards us for a bit, then lazily crept up to a water jump and started **rolling around** in a puddle.

The judges did not look impressed.

Dad tried his best to get Superdog to go over a jump. Superdog just looked up at Dad **blankly** and **wriggled** a bit.

At this point his tail fell off.

I looked to Dad for ideas, but he was just **FACEPALMING** himself.

Percy and I looked up at the judges who were staring at us now with a look of anger and **bewilderment**.

We stared back with a look of embarrassment.

At least nothing else could go wrong, right?

WRONG!

Superdog had a *sudden* and *unexpected* attack of rage. He bounded over to the sidelines where the other chameleons were waiting quietly to compete, and started chasing them and trying to lick them. Dad tried to catch Superdog while other people attempted to rescue their **ESCAPING CHAMELEONS** ...

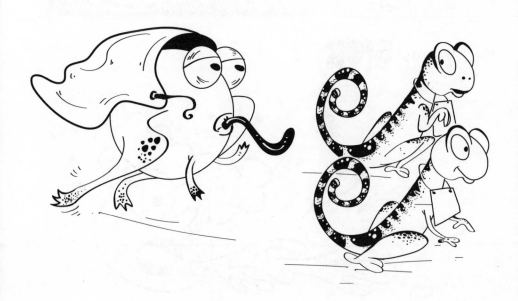

I let out a **loud fart** ...

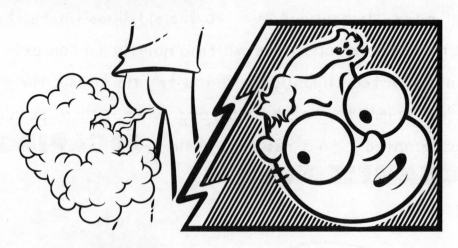

Percy was **SICK** ...

We were disqualified.

I ran over and grabbed Superdog, then Dad, Percy and I **LEGGED IT!**

We managed to make it to the car and escape the **SCREAMING** mob. On the way home Dad suggested that we tell Mum that we'd decided NOT to enter and that we should never speak of it again.

LET'S NOT TELL YOUR MOTHER ABOUT THIS.

I can't believe that Ms Mills actually turned up at Science Club today, this can't be good!

She's **EVERYWHERE** these days:

—In PE class

-In jiu-jitsu

-Now in Science Club

... What next?

She didn't say too much, she just sat in a corner **SPYiNG** on us and occasionally talking to Mr Hammond about showing him some moves. It was **REALLY AWKWARD**.

Mr Hammond looked uncomfortable and a bit **sweaty** during the whole class. In any case he got on with the main point, which was showing all of us the finished robot design.

It looked AWESOME!!

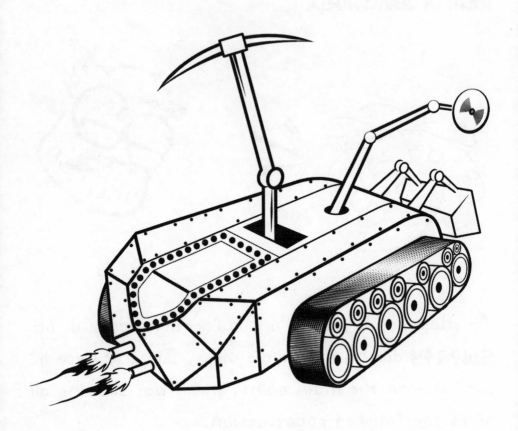

From Leo and Michael's design he has kept the **flamethrower**, he's used quite a lot of Amy and Debra's ideas, and he's MiXED Neil and Belinda's and Gareth's designs, giving the robot a rotating blade on one arm.

Percy and I did the best though: Mr Hammond has decided that he'll keep the name from our design, so the robot will be called the Mighty Iron Foot!! Percy and I felt very PROUD.

(And a bit **gassy.**)

Apparently the whole class has to build the **robot** together.

-    Amy and Debra will do all the welding and the wheelbase.

-    Gareth is going to do the electrics (or his dad is, more to the point).

-    Leo, Neil, Belinda, Percy and I get to take care of the best part: the **DECORATION!**

Ms Mills kept asking what she could do. Mr Hammond kept saying that he couldn't think of anything.

I hope she doesn't come back again!
I got home to find that Granny Jean and Grandad

Leonard had come around for tea. I hadn't seen them for a while and they were very excited to hear all about the **ROBOT RIOT** competition.

WHEN IS IT?

WHERE IS IT?

WILL THERE BE ALIENS?

CAN WE DRESS UP?

Mum seemed annoyed, but that was probably because Dad and I had been secretly **EXPERIMENTING** with his fart jellies and potions. She told us we were ruining dinner.

Also, she may have found out about Superdog

ruining the **CHAMELEON GYMKHANA**. It was in the local newspaper, apparently. Mr Nesbit brought her a copy when he came round to complain about Lucy-Fur digging up his dead chameleon *yet again*. Anyway ... Mum probably had more than one reason to seem annoyed.

I was just biting into a sausage when Dad let out a **SQUEAKER**.

NRRRRR . . .
SQUEEEEEEEKKKK . . .

It was **HiLARiOUS**.

Mum was horrified.

THAT'S IT!
YOU HAVE BEEN TOLD BEFORE: ANYONE WHO FARTS AT THE DINNER TABLE CAN GO OUTSIDE AND EAT IN THE GARDEN!

I didn't think it was fair for Dad to have to go outside on his own, so I let one out, then picked up my plate and followed him outside. We made our way to the clubhouse where we were joined shortly afterwards by Grandad Leonard, and then by Granny Jean.

Granny Jean and Grandad Leonard wanted to see our robot design. They wanted to know if it could go into space.

I showed Granny and Grandad our design. They really liked all the **FLASHING** lights and the farting, but they were unimpressed by the lack of **PHASERS**.

WHERE ARE THE PHASERS?

TYPICAL!!! They always want more **PHASERS**!!!!

Granny Jean said that we should teach the robot some **martial arts**.

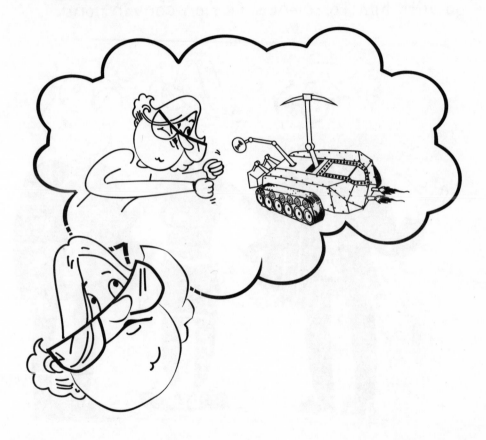

I explained that Ms Mills was already trying that, and told them all about how she kept on harassing Mr Hammond.

Granny and Grandad weren't happy. They're **FRiENDS** with Mr Hammond and they sometimes go with him to science-fiction conventions.

Either way, Granny Jean and Grandad Leonard were really excited about **ROBOT RIOT** and asked me if I could get them tickets to the show.

Science Club has been FARTASTIC recently!
A lot of work has gone into the Mighty Iron Foot.
We've all worked really hard!

Debra Derby created a phenomenal rotating
wheelbase, the armour and weapons have been
EXPERTLY HANDCRAFTED by Amy Almond and
everyone in the team has really pulled together.
Even Gareth has been less of a twit than usual!

We've added FLASHING UFO-style lights and a flamethrower.

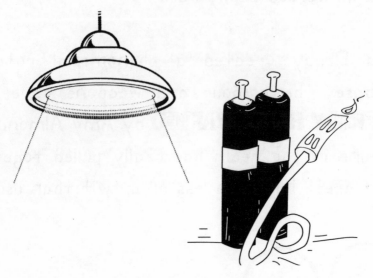

We were all very disappointed that we couldn't make the robot fart, but we all agreed that Dad could make a special fart jelly so that at least all the team members can fart the whole way through the competition.

RESULT!!

The competition is to be held in the next town over, in **Burnington High School.** All the schools from the area will be competing for a place in the national championships.

We know that competition will be tough, as Burnington won last year's **ROBOT RIOT** and they always have cutting-edge technology. Their robot is sponsored by Acmetech, the company that **SLIGHTLY-LESS-TWIT-FACED-THAN-USUAL** Gareth Trumpshaw's dad works for. So we know that they **DEFiNiTELY** cheat.

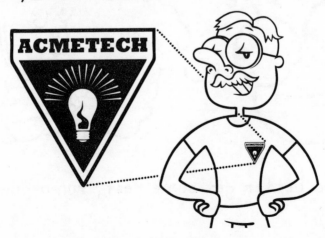

Anyway, it all kicks off tomorrow! Leo's mum has very kindly offered to take us all in her ice cream van as Mr Norton, the headmaster, borrowed the school bus for a camping trip.

RESULT!!

I mean, **fighting robots** and ice cream ... can the day get any better?

Right, I'd better get some rest, tomorrow's the
BIG DAY!

We arrived at Burnington High School very early this morning. Although it wasn't too early to have **ice cream** for breakfast ... even though Percy went a funny colour and puked *pistachio ice cream* all over his cast ...

Why, Percy, **why?!**

We were led around the school building and the playing field to the school gym. There, at the entrance, we were all given **badges** with our team name and shown to an area of the gym that had been prepared for our team. In the centre of the gym there was a sort of ring that had been built *especially for the occasion.*

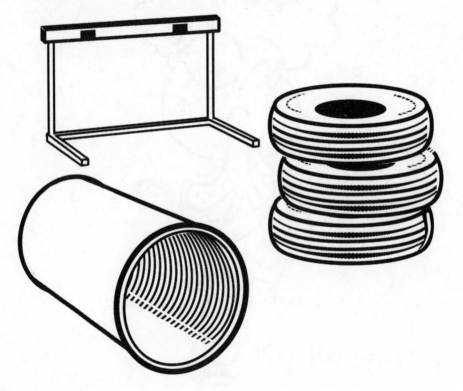

It was sealed off from the audience for **SAFETY REASONS** and it was raised. There was a variety of obstacles, like tyres for the robots to bounce off, booby traps made out of bits of old power tools and food blenders. There was even a **FLAME PIT** which seemed to have been made from an old gas barbeque. It was the **MOST AWESOME THING EVER!**

There was a real atmosphere in the gym too!
And with lights and cameras set up, it was like a
HUGE sporting event!

We all got very nervous
when we started to see the
other teams turning up with
their robots.

They looked very **SCARY**
and impressive.
The robots all had different
defence and attack systems.

Some of them were designed to flip other robots over, some had **big weapons** like ice picks and hammers, and a lot of them had rotating blades to saw through the other robots' armour.

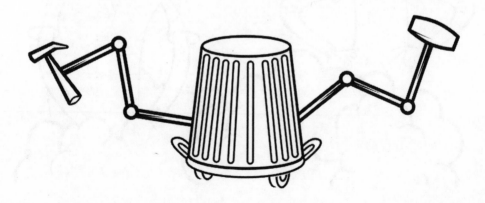

I looked over at Mr Hammond. He looked a bit nervous.

I offered him some **fart jelly**. He took some.

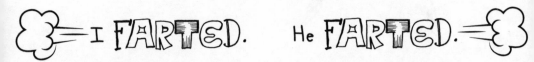

I FARTED.   He FARTED.

We both felt better.

A referee got up on a stand and explained the competition rules to all the teams.

Apparently all the robots would be **paired up** randomly against another robot in round one. Then the winning robot from each round would be matched up against another winning robot and the losers of each round would be **DISQUALIFIED** ... and so on until there were only two robots left to go head to head.

It was a lot of pressure: it meant that we couldn't lose a single round.

I looked over at the Burnington team. Their robot was the best robot by far. It looked like a **spaceship!**

And ... I couldn't believe it! Gareth Trumpshaw's dad was there with them! What a **TRAITOR!!!**

How could he be working for the Burnington team when his son was with Greenville?

I noticed Gareth looking **disappointed** and felt a bit sorry for him. After all, not everyone can have an awesome, FARTASTIC dad like mine!

I even ...

YOU WON'T BELIEVE THIS!

I even went over to Gareth Trumpshaw and offered him some of Dad's **fart jelly**.

He seemed to cheer up a bit.

Then he did a really **twitty** fart. (Just because I gave him jelly doesn't mean I don't still think he's a twit!)

PHHHHHHRT....

Our first battle was against Olsen Secondary School. It was **TENSE**.

Olsen Secondary School had a good reputation and their robot was really **FLAT**. The idea behind their design was for their robot to be able to get underneath the opponents' robot and flip it over.

The referee called our teams and we were each told to take our place at opposite ends of the arena. Gareth Trumpshaw wanted to be the one controlling our robot, but Mr Hammond said:

NO WAY, I'VE BEEN WAITING FOR THIS MOMENT MY WHOLE LIFE!

He was not going to let anyone crush his dream.

I saw the look of a madman in Mr Hammond's eyes and I knew that he would be too focused on controlling the robot to be able to organise the team. That was a job for **EXPERIMENTAL FACE!**

We needed to organise ourselves so we could be ready for any emergency!

NEIL, BELINDA, LEO, MICHAEL, WE NEED YOU TO CRUSH THE OTHER TEAMS' SPIRIT. WE NEED YOU TO CHEER ON THE MIGHTY IRON FOOT AND LET THE OTHER TEAM KNOW THAT THEIR ROBOT IS RUBBISH!

YEAH!!!! GO IRON FOOT!!!

Then I looked at Gareth and Percy. I hated saying this, but I knew it was the best thing for the team:

Everyone took their positions (except Gareth for some reason), as Mr Hammond led the team into battle.

The robot arena was full of rotating blades, traps, fire pits ... you had to try to back your opponents' robot into anything that could DAMAGE it.

Each robot-driving team was in a cabin at the opposite end of the hall. The audience was all around the arena.

I spotted Granny Jean and Grandad Leonard as they arrived ... **IN FULL SCI-FI COSTUME!!**

Ugh!! Why are relatives ALWAYS  so **embarrassing?** I pretended that I hadn't seen them, but then Mr Hammond spotted them.

He waved and shouted:

HEY, LOOK DANNY!!
IT'S YOUR GRANDPARENTS!!
LET'S ALL GIVE THEM A BIG WAVE!

The whole of Science Club turned around and waved at my grandparents. Then they turned back and they sniggered at me. I must have THE MOST **embarrassing** family out of all the kids at school!!!

Fortunately just then, round one started:

OLSEN'S STINGRAY
VS.
GREENVILLE'S MIGHTY IRON FOOT

The countdown started. Both teams stood tensely in their corners, controllers in hand, waiting anxiously to make the first move.

Five,
four,
three,
two,
one ...

THE BELL RANG!

The Stingray came flying out of its corner. It made a beeline for **THE MIGHTY IRON FOOT**, diving straight underneath our robot and flipping it upside down. We all panicked.

Mr Hammond masterfully flicked a switch and our robot was back on its feet (well, its wheels) in no time. **Hydraulic arms to the rescue!**

Mr Hammond meant business! He turned the robot around, then, having forced the Stingray into a corner, he dropped the rotating blade on it and cut the robot in half like a **sandwich**.

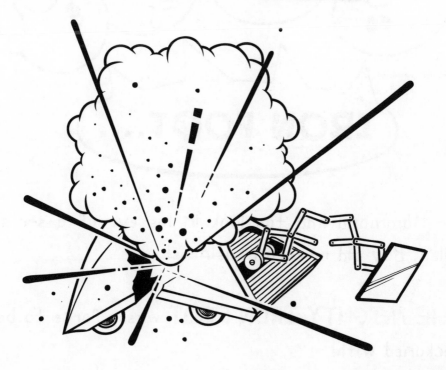

Our team cheered: **IRON FOOT, IRON FOOT, IRON FOOT!!!** The crowd went wild!!

IRON FOOT.....

Mr Hammond had the look in his eye of a serial killer. Boy did he mean business!

THE MIGHTY IRON FOOT was a force to be reckoned with!

We came up against some **PRETTY FiERCE** robots in the following rounds, but Iron Foot was on fire!! The team was on fire!! Mr Hammond was on fire!!

He laughed like a madman as he SMASHED, shredded, flipped and hacked the competition to pieces!

It was amazing to watch. We **booed** all of our opponents and cheered and farted victoriously every time we won a round!

By the end of the afternoon the audience was cheering and chanting along with us:

IRON FOOT, IRON FOOT, IRON FOOT!!!

We stopped for a technical break. The teams were all given time to make repairs and small adjustments to their robots (and in our case, to wolf down some ice cream and FART JELLY) as the judges prepared to announce the final round.

I supervised Debra and Amy as they worked against the clock, **sweating buckets**. They were welding and repairing the Mighty Iron Foot.

Mr Hammond rested in a corner. He looked like he'd
been in a war, but nothing could kill his confidence.

COME ON,
MIGHTY IRON FOOT!

The judges finally came back on stage. Everyone
gathered around and grew quiet.

"So ... ahem, ahem ..." (A judge coughed into the crackling microphone.)

The crowd **cheered** in excitement.

I looked over at Mr Hammond. He looked a bit **SCARED** ...

I looked over at Gareth. He looked a bit **gutted**.

I felt a bit sorry for him, so I offered him some more **FART JELLY** to make him feel better.

I was secretly worried that Gareth might have given his dad **TOP SECRET** technical information about our robot. After all, he clearly gets his **twittish** behaviour from his dad, so maybe being a cheater runs in the family too. We could be at a **SERIOUS** disadvantage!

We were coming to the end of our break. Mr Hammond looked a bit **nervous** as he checked that everything was still working while Amy Almond performed emergency welding repairs. The Mighty Iron Foot was beginning to look like a FRANKENROBOT!

After a few tense minutes the judges announced,

STAND BY, TEAMS ...
FIVE MINUTES TILL COMBAT.

Greenville Science Club team huddled up. Mr Hammond spoke:

TEAM,
YOU'VE BEEN THE BEST SCIENCE CLUB
I'VE EVER HAD THE PRIVILEGE OF TEACHING.
WE'VE GOT ALL THE WAY TO THE FINALS,
WE'VE ROCKED IT SO FAR . . .
SO LET'S ALL EAT SOME OF THIS FARTASTIC
JELLY THAT DANNY BROUGHT WITH HIM
AND GO OUT WITH A BLAST!

And as we made our way back to the arena one last time, I let out a small, nervous FART of expectation.

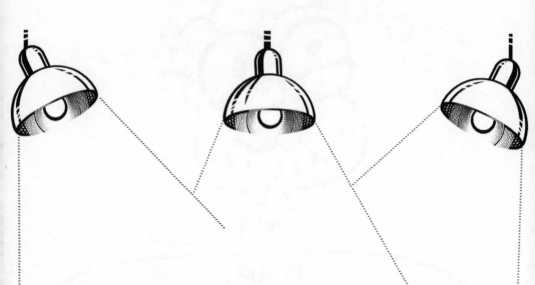

The tension was high for the final round. The lights had been dimmed, we had red and blue search lights hovering over the arena and a smoke machine gave the event a really **DRAMATIC** effect.

As the referee announced:

TEAMS, ON YOUR MARKS ...

DISASTER STRUCK!!!!!!!

Ms Mills had crept into our corner and was making her way towards Mr Hammond!! **WHY????!!!!**

Suddenly there was Ms Mills, right behind Mr Hammond.

Burnington's Cremator was heading towards **THE MIGHTY IRON FOOT** with rotating flaming blades while Mr Hammond was ... **wrestling!!!** What on Earth was going on?!

Ms Mills was trying to wrestle the controller out of Mr Hammond's hands, shouting things like: "I'll save the day, leave it to me!" and "This is a job for Tank Girl!" but Mr Hammond was not going to go down without a fight.

With all the commotion Mr Hammond suddenly lost his grip on the controller . . . that's when Gareth **JUMPED** in and snatched the controller out of mid-air ...

Now, normally I don't like Gareth Trumpshaw very much, but if it hadn't been for him, our robot would have been **ROASTED** by this stage.

Gareth managed to dodge all the other robot's manoeuvres and even get in a few good hits ... so I guess he has learnt something from his dad building the robot for the enemy team!

We all **screamed** and **cheered** for all we were worth. Gareth was fighting hard, but he was no match for his dad's years of expertise ... and when the Cremator got **IRON FOOT** against a fence, I thought it was all over.

At that moment I spotted Granny Jean jumping over chairs and **CHARGING** towards us.

Before you knew it, Granny Jean was in our corner and she'd backed Ms Mills up against a wall.

Ms Mills just looked annoyed and amused.

LISTEN GRANDMA, I DON'T KNOW WHAT YOUR PROBLEM IS, BUT I'D GO BACK TO YOUR KNITTING NOW IF I WERE YOU. I HAVE A BLACK BELT IN JIU-JITSU . . . OR WOULD YOU LIKE TO FIND OUT ABOUT THAT THE HARD WAY?

Ms Mills had said enough.

Granny Jean looked like she was going to shyly retire back to her seat, then surprised Ms Mills with a **spinning kick** to the chin, knocking her to the ground before she put her into an **ARMLOCK**.

I guess that was the moment Ms Mills found out the hard way that Granny Jean also has a black belt in **jiu-jitsu** ... and **kenpo** ... and **taekwondo** ...

Anyway, with Ms Mills under control, Mr Hammond was back in the game.

Gareth handed the controller back to Mr Hammond, but there was no disguising the fact that the Mighty Iron Foot was in **huge trouble**.

Gareth had done his best, but our robot was **seriously damaged**: the spinning disc had stopped spinning, the flamethrower wasn't working, and the hydraulic flipping arm was jammed.

Our robot could still move and dodge attacks, but our weapons had been **DESTROYED!!!**

The Cremator moved backwards towards its corner. It was clear that it was preparing to make one final **ALMIGHTY** charge to finish us off. As it started to gather speed and steam towards us with rotating, flaming circular saws, we knew we were DOOMED.

After all that hard work, it was hard to believe that Ms Mills could come along and **ruin** it in a few minutes!

We all put our hands over our eyes so as not to witness **THE MIGHTY IRON FOOT'S** final moments.

All except for Gareth, who stood in disbelief as his dad's robot prepared to **CRUSH** ours, and Mr Hammond, who stared in concentration as the Cremator shot towards our robot.

As we felt the **FLAMES** get closer, we suddenly heard Mr Hammond shout:

IT'S TIME FOR THE SECRET WEAPON!!!

When the Cremator was almost on top of **IRON FOOT**, Mr Hammond pushed a button. A compartment opened at the top of our robot and a huge iron foot came down, **CRUSHING** the Cremator into the ground!!

We all had to take a second look, it happened so fast!

As the smoke cleared, the **crushed** and **crackling** remains of Burnington's Cremator were now **SQUASHED** under the **unholy weight** of the Mighty Iron Foot.

As the Cremator sparked and whirred, the referee started to count: 4-3-2-1 ...

REFEREE: Ladies and gentlemen ... it's a knockout!!

It took a few seconds to sink in. Suddenly the crowd started **cheering** ... and we all had the same realisation!

WE HAD WON! THE MIGHTY IRON FOOT HAD WON! GREENVILLE SCIENCE CLUB HAD WON!

Mr Hammond was so happy that he was almost crying.

Granny Jean and Ms Mills stopped beating each other up and started hugging each other and cheering.

I looked around at the team I had put together and led to victory; all the kids huddled together and started jumping up and down – EVEN Gareth Trumpshaw!

Percy was so excited that he was **SICK**. No surprises there!

I felt a little emotional knowing that I, the great **EXPERIMENTAL FACE**, had taken charge ... like a general ... or a king ... leading his troops into battle. Because they all believed in me, we had won. **WE HAD WON THE WAR!!**

And then the judges announced:

> LADIES AND GENTLEMEN,
> GREENVILLE'S MIGHTY IRON
> FOOT HAS DEMONSTRATED
> ITS WORTHINESS AND WILL BE INVITED
> ALONG WITH THE WHOLE TEAM
> TO SPEND A WEEK IN LONDON,
> WHERE THE MIGHTY IRON FOOT WILL
> COMPETE IN THE NATIONAL FINALS.
> GOOD LUCK, GREENVILLE,
> A WELL-DESERVED VICTORY!

We all cheered again: we were going to LONDON!! This was huge news for the Science Club! What a day! What a team! Never before in Greenville history had our school reached the finals of anything! And to get to the finals with THE MIGHTY IRON FOOT? A robot that I had single-handedly named, BY MYSELF (with some help from Percy, although it was almost all my idea).

The whole town would finally have to recognise my GENIUS, **SUPERHERO-**
Like inventing skills!

The team felt like more than just a team as we packed away our stuff. We weren't just a troop of **SUPER-SKILLED** inventors, we were friends.

Even Gareth Trumpshaw, despite still being a massive **twit**, had shown that he could sometimes make a small effort to help us defeat the **enemy**. I decided that maybe I could forget he was my nemesis for the rest of the day, seeing as it was a special occasion.

And then we had the best news ever: Leo's mum said that as a **special prize** we could go back to the ice cream van and have all the ice cream we could eat!!

What an **AWESOME** end to an **awesome** day.

Well ... provided you're not sitting next to an ice-cream-filled **PUKING** Percy on the way home!